Leap Frog

Tracy Kompelien

Illustrated by Anne Haberstroh

Consulting Editor, Diane Craig, M.A./Reading Specialist

ABDO
Publishing Company

Published by ABDO Publishing Company, 4940 Viking Drive, Edina, Minnesota 55435.

Printed in the United States.

Credits
Edited by: Pam Price
Curriculum Coordinator: Nancy Tuminelly
Cover and Interior Design and Production: Mighty Media
Photo Credits: AbleStock, ShutterStock

Library of Congress Cataloging-in-Publication Data

Kompelien, Tracy, 1975-
    Leap frog / Tracy Kompelien; illustrated by Anne Haberstroh.
       p. cm. -- (Fact & fiction. Critter chronicles)
    Summary: Two frog friends, Fred and Floyd, compete in an international frog competition. Alternating pages provide facts about frogs.
    ISBN 10 1-59928-448-0 (hardcover)
    ISBN 10 1-59928-449-9 (paperback)

    ISBN 13 978-1-59928-448-4 (hardcover)
    ISBN 13 978-1-59928-449-1 (paperback)
    [1. Racing--Fiction. 2. Jumping--Fiction. 3. Contests--Fiction. 4. Frogs--Fiction.] I. Haberstroh, Anne, ill. II. Title. III. Series.

    PZ7.K83497Lea 2006
    [E]--dc22

                                                                                    2006005542

SandCastle Level: Fluent

SandCastle™ books are created by a professional team of educators, reading specialists, and content developers around five essential components—phonemic awareness, phonics, vocabulary, text comprehension, and fluency—to assist young readers as they develop reading skills and strategies and increase their general knowledge. All books are written, reviewed, and leveled for guided reading, early reading intervention, and Accelerated Reader® programs for use in shared, guided, and independent reading and writing activities to support a balanced approach to literacy instruction. The SandCastle™ series has four levels that correspond to early literacy development. The levels help teachers and parents select appropriate books for young readers.

Emerging Readers
(no flags)

Beginning Readers
(1 flag)

Transitional Readers
(2 flags)

Fluent Readers
(3 flags)

These levels are meant only as a guide. All levels are subject to change.

FACT & FICTION

This series provides early fluent readers the opportunity to develop reading comprehension strategies and increase fluency. These books are appropriate for guided, shared, and independent reading.

FACT The left-hand pages incorporate realistic photographs to enhance readers' understanding of informational text.

FICTION The right-hand pages engage readers with an entertaining, narrative story that is supported by whimsical illustrations.

The Fact and Fiction pages can be read separately to improve comprehension through questioning, predicting, making inferences, and summarizing. They can also be read side-by-side, in spreads, which encourages students to explore and examine different writing styles.

FACT OR FICTION? This fun quiz helps reinforce students' understanding of what is real and not real.

SPEED READ The text-only version of each section includes word-count rulers for fluency practice and assessment.

GLOSSARY Higher-level vocabulary and concepts are defined in the glossary.

SandCastle™ would like to hear from you.

Tell us your stories about reading this book. What was your favorite page? Was there something hard that you needed help with? Share the ups and downs of learning to read. To get posted on the ABDO Publishing Company Web site, send us an e-mail at:

sandcastle@abdopublishing.com

Frogs have webbed feet and long legs, which help them to jump and swim.

The Leapfrog Leap-a-Long, the largest international frog competition, is near. Frogs from all over the world come to Lily Pad Lake to show off their leaping talents.

To protect their thin skin from being dried out by sun and heat, most frogs are active at night and rest during the day.

Every Saturday morning, Fred wakes up at the crack of dawn. He eats his protein bar, has a cup of coffee, and hops down to Lily Pad Lake. Fred has entered the Leapfrog Leap-a-Long and is training for the big day.

Except for the very coldest places, such as Antarctica and the Arctic, frogs are found in most parts of the world.

"One, two, three, four …,"
he counts as he does
his training.

Meanwhile, in South
America, Fred's best friend,
Floyd, is also training.
He can't wait to compete
against Fred.

9

Frog species are very diverse, coming in a wide range of colors and sizes.

Ready for the race,
Fred grabs his sweatband
and heads toward Lily Pad
Lake. As Fred is hopping over
the tall hill, he stops and looks
below. He sees a beautiful array
of colors moving and mingling.

11

Poisonous frogs are often brightly colored.
This warns predators that it is dangerous
to eat them.

Fred spots his unusually bright blue friend, Floyd. Fred says, "Hey, Floyd, it's been a long time!"

Many frogs sit on lily pads in order to catch insects as they fly by or land on the water.

START

Fred and Floyd line up at the first pad.
They have trained together many times,
but this is their first race against each
other. They smile nervously as the
starter's gun goes off.

Frogs usually swallow their food whole.
Most frogs eat insects and worms,
although some eat tadpoles, small fish,
and small animals.

Fred and Floyd leap smoothly, never missing a lily pad. They are neck and neck until Floyd is distracted by a juicy-looking fly. He can't help darting out his tongue to catch it.

Frogs do not drink water. Instead, they absorb it through their skin.

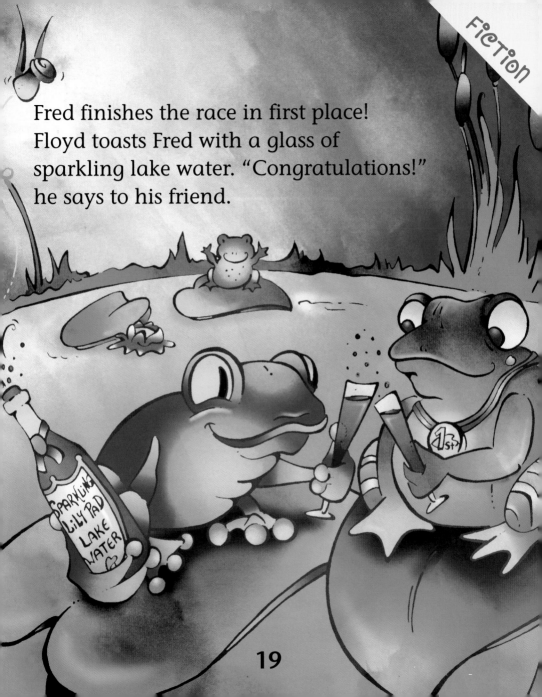

Fred finishes the race in first place!
Floyd toasts Fred with a glass of
sparkling lake water. "Congratulations!"
he says to his friend.

Read each statement below. Then decide whether it's from the FACT section or the FiCTiON section!

1. Frogs eat protein bars for breakfast.

2. Frogs wear sweatbands.

3. Some frogs are brightly colored.

4. Frogs usually swallow their food whole.

ANSWERS
1. fiction 2. fiction 3. fact 4. fact

Frogs have webbed feet and long legs, which help them to jump and swim.

9
14

To protect their thin skin from being dried out by sun and heat, most frogs are active at night and rest during the day.

24
35
38

Except for the very coldest places, such as Antarctica and the Arctic, frogs are found in most parts of the world.

46
56
59

Frog species are very diverse, coming in a wide range of colors and sizes.

68
73

Poisonous frogs are often brightly colored. This warns predators that it is dangerous to eat them.

80
89

Many frogs sit on lily pads in order to catch insects as they fly by or land on the water.

100
109

Frogs usually swallow their food whole. Most frogs eat insects and worms, although some eat tadpoles, small fish, and small animals.

117
125
130

Frogs do not drink water. Instead, they absorb it through their skin.

139
142

The Leapfrog Leap-a-Long, the largest international frog competition, is near. Frogs from all over the world come to Lily Pad Lake to show off their leaping talents.

Every Saturday morning, Fred wakes up at the crack of dawn. He eats his protein bar, has a cup of coffee, and hops down to Lily Pad Lake. Fred has entered the Leapfrog Leap-a-Long and is training for the big day.

"One, two, three, four …," he counts as he does his training.

Meanwhile, in South America, Fred's best friend, Floyd, is also training. He can't wait to compete against Fred.

Ready for the race, Fred grabs his sweatband and heads toward Lily Pad Lake. As Fred is hopping over the tall hill, he stops and looks below. He sees a beautiful array of colors moving and mingling.

7
13
24
29
37
48
58
67
72
81
83
89
98
101
109
118
127
136
138

Fred spots his unusually bright blue friend, Floyd. 146
Fred says, "Hey, Floyd, it's been a long time!" 155

Fred and Floyd line up at the first pad. They have 166
trained together many times, but this is their first 175
race against each other. They smile nervously as 183
the starter's gun goes off. 188

Fred and Floyd leap smoothly, never missing a 196
lily pad. They are neck and neck until Floyd is 206
distracted by a juicy-looking fly. He can't help 215
darting out his tongue to catch it. 222

Fred finishes the race in first place! Floyd toasts 231
Fred with a glass of sparkling lake water. 239
"Congratulations!" he says to his friend. 245

GLOSSARY

distract. to cause to turn away form one's original focus of interest

diverse. differing from one another

international. involving more than one nation

leap. to jump or spring up from something

mingle. to mix together without losing the identifying characteristics of the individuals

poisonous. containing a substance that can injure or kill

species. a group of related living beings